Catch, Patch!

Written by Alice Russ Watson
Illustrated by Leesh Li

Collins

Who and what is in this story?

Listen and say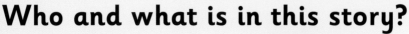

basketball

Jay

Candy

Download the audio at www.collins.co.uk/839767

computer game

Patch

football

🎧 Jay is at home. He wants to play basketball.

Jay asks, "Hi Candy! What are you doing?"

"Do you want to play basketball with me?"

Candy says, "I'm playing a computer game. I don't want to play basketball."

Jay is sad. He says, "But I want to play basketball."

Candy says, "Jay! I don't want to play basketball! Go and play with the cat."

Jay asks, "Can cats play basketball?"

Jay says, "Hi Patch! What are you doing? Do you want to play basketball with me?"

Patch looks at the ball but she
doesn't understand.

Jay throws the ball to Patch.

Catch!

Crash! The ball hits the window and Patch jumps.

Jay catches the ball.

Patch is sitting at the bathroom door.

Jay tries again. He throws the ball.

Patch!
Catch the ball!

The ball goes in the bathroom.

Splash! Oh no! The ball is in the baby's bath!

Oh, Jay!

Sorry, Mum.

Jay cleans the floor. He looks at Patch and his ball. He says, "Now what?"

Look! Patch kicks the ball to Jay.
Jay is very happy.

Jay says, "Cats can't play basketball but my cat can play football!"

Picture dictionary

Listen and repeat

catch

hit

jump

kick

play

throw

1 Look and order the story

2 Listen and say

Collins

Published by Collins
An imprint of HarperCollins*Publishers*
Westerhill Road
Bishopbriggs
Glasgow
G64 2QT

HarperCollins*Publishers*
1st Floor, Watermarque Building
Ringsend Road
Dublin 4
Ireland

William Collins' dream of knowledge for all began with the publication of his first book in 1819.

A self-educated mill worker, he not only enriched millions of lives, but also founded a flourishing publishing house. Today, staying true to this spirit, Collins books are packed with inspiration, innovation and practical expertise. They place you at the centre of a world of possibility and give you exactly what you need to explore it.

© HarperCollins*Publishers* Limited 2020

10 9 8 7 6 5 4 3 2

ISBN 978-0-00-839767-8

Collins® and COBUILD® are registered trademarks of HarperCollins*Publishers* Limited

www.collins.co.uk/elt

British Library Cataloguing in Publication Data

A catalogue record for this publication is available from the British Library.

Author: Alice Russ Watson
Illustrator: Leesh Li (Beehive)
Series editor: Rebecca Adlard
Publishing manager: Lisa Todd
Product managers: Jennifer Hall and Caroline Green
In-house editor: Alma Puts Keren
Project manager: Emily Hooton
Editor: Deborah Friedland
Proofreaders: Natalie Murray and Michael Lamb
Cover designer: Kevin Robbins
Typesetter: 2Hoots Publishing Services Ltd
Audio produced by id audio, London
Reading guide author: Sarah Jane Lewis-Mantzaris
Production controller: Rachel Weaver
Printed and bound by: GPS Group, Slovenia

Download the audio for this book and a reading guide for parents and teachers at www.collins.co.uk/839767